PHOTOGRAPHY CREDITS: 2 (c) ©Oleg Znamenskiy/Fotolia; 3 (c) ©Artville/Getty Images; 3 (r) ©Artville/Getty Images; 4 (l) Leaves: © PhotoDisc/Getty Images; 4 (c) Artville/Getty Images; 4 (r) ©James and James/Getty Images; 6 (r) ©Ocean/Corbis; 6 (r) ©Scott Camazine/Alamy Images; 6 (r) ©Wataru Yanagida/Digital Vision/Getty Images; 6 (c) ©John Kaprielian/Science Source; 7 (l) ©Per Magnus Persson/Johnér Images/Corbis; 7 (c) ©Ocean/Corbis; 7 (r) ©Simone Mueller/The Image Bank/Getty Images

Copyright © by Houghton Mifflin Harcourt Publishing Company

All rights reserved. No part of this work may be reproduced or transmitted in any form or by any means, electronic or mechanical, including photocopying or recording, or by any information storage and retrieval system, without the prior written permission of the copyright owner unless such copying is expressly permitted by federal copyright law. Requests for permission to make copies of any part of the work should be addressed to Houghton Mifflin Harcourt Publishing Company, Attn: Contracts, Copyrights, and Licensing, 9400 Southpark Center Loop, Orlando, Florida 32819-8647.

Printed in U.S.A.

ISBN: 978-0-544-07197-1

5 6 7 8 9 10 1083 21 20 19 18 17 16 15 14

4500470117   A B C D E F G

If you have received these materials as examination copies free of charge, Houghton Mifflin Harcourt Publishing Company retains title to the materials and they may not be resold. Resale of examination copies is strictly prohibited.

Possession of this publication in print format does not entitle users to convert this publication, or any portion of it, into electronic format.

What Are Plants?

HOUGHTON MIFFLIN HARCOURT

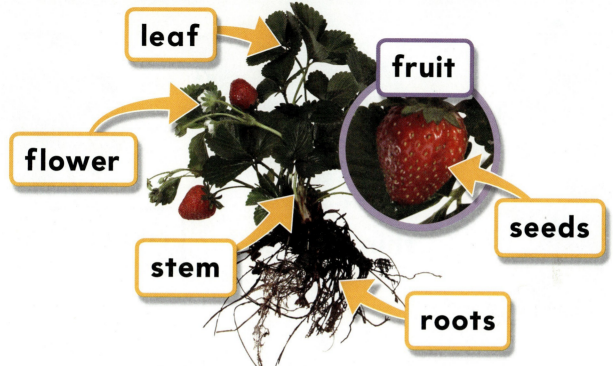

A plant has roots, a stem, and leaves.
It may have flowers, fruit, and seeds.

What are a plant's parts?

Leaves have different shapes.
We can sort plants by the shape of their leaves.

A plant needs light and air.
It also needs water, soil, and space to grow.

What does a plant need?

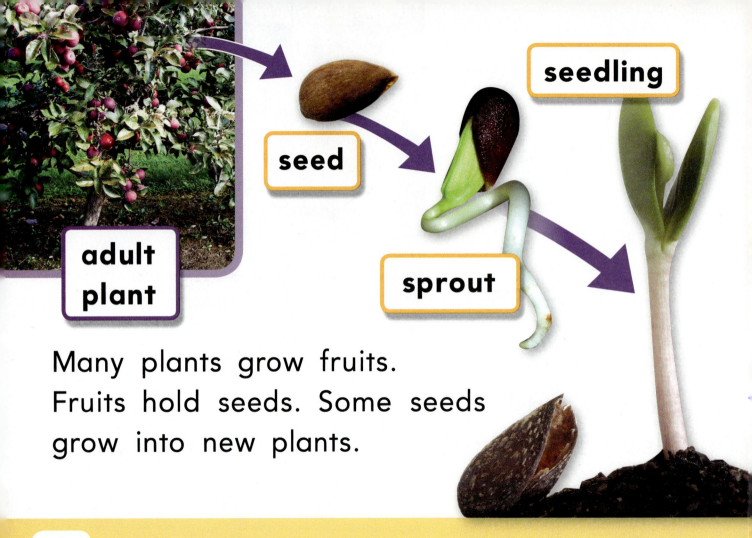

Many plants grow fruits. Fruits hold seeds. Some seeds grow into new plants.

new plant

growing plant

adult plant

The new plant looks like the adult plant.
The plant grows to be an adult plant, too.
The new plant looks like its parent plant.

Responding

Identify Plant Parts

Bring a potted plant into the classroom or take children outside to a plant around the schoolyard. Have children observe the plant and identify its roots, stem, leaves, and other visible parts. Then have students draw a picture of the plant and label the parts.

How a Plant Grows

Have children write a summary of information in the text by copying and completing the following sentences. Have them draw a picture to go with each sentence.

A seed comes from a(n) _____.

Seeds need _____, _____, and _____.

The plant begins as a(n) _____.

Next it becomes a(n) _____.

Finally, it becomes a(n) _____.

Vocabulary

adult plant	seeds
air	shrub
flower	soil
fruit	space to grow
leaf	sprout
light	stem
roots	tree
seedling	